Sweet Dreams

Contents

No One
Like You

8

Ruff was hungry. A huge grumble rumbled around his tummy. He could hear Rufus clattering around in the kitchen. A delicious smell of freshly baked cupcakes sailed past his nose. "Yummy," thought Ruff.

9

Ruff skipped into the kitchen — Rufus was tidying up "Would you like some help?" asked Ruff. "I could try one of those cupcakes for you."

"Oh, really!" said Rufus, smiling.

10

11

"No one makes cakes like you," said Ruff.

13

Ruff was bored. He twiddled his fingers, tapped his toes, and twiddled his fingers again. He had no one to play with.

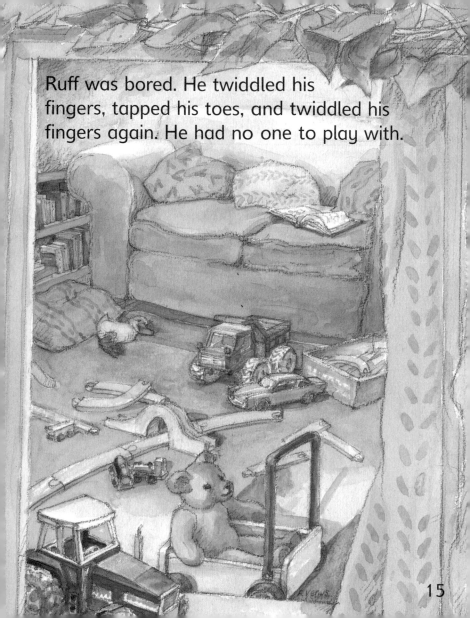

15

Later, Ruff tiptoed back into the living room —
Rufus was reading.

"Would you like something better to read?"
asked Ruff. "I could find you an exciting story."

"Oh, really!" said Rufus, smiling.

"No one tells a story like you," said Ruff.

19

Ruff was annoyed. He was trying to make a model car. He fiddled and twiddled and fiddled, but he couldn't put it together.
Then he had an idea!

21

Ruff galloped out to the garden—Rufus was working.

"Would you like something fun to do?" asked Ruff. "I could let you help me with my model car."

"Oh, really!" said Rufus, smiling.

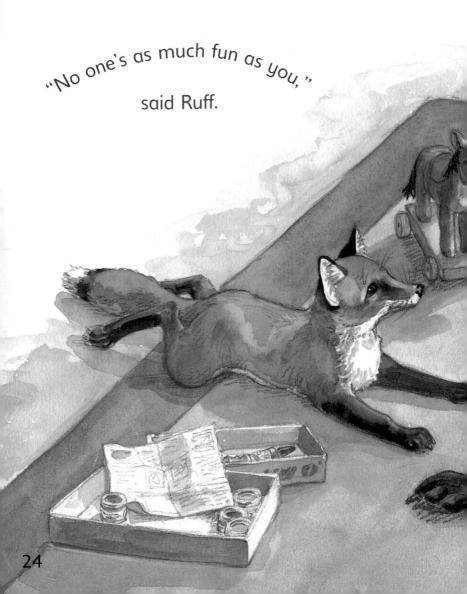

"No one's as much fun as you,"

said Ruff.

25

It was bedtime! Rufus tucked Ruff into bed. Ruff was feeling scared. He didn't like the shadows that flickered all round — it was very quiet.

Then he had an idea!

Ruff crept out of his bedroom and into Rufus's room.

Rufus was snoring loudly. It made Ruff giggle and woke Rufus up.

"Would you like someone to cuddle?" asked Ruff. "I'm very good at cuddling."

"Oh, really!" said Rufus, smiling.

"No one cuddles like you,"

yawned Ruff, climbing into
Rufus's bed.

30

31

"Oh, really!" said Rufus...

"Well, no one loves you as much as I do, because there's no one like you." 33

If You Hold My Hand

Oakey's mom opened the front door.
"Come on, Oakey. Let's go outside
and explore."

ROSE
COTTAGE

But Oakey wasn't really sure. He was only
small, and the world looked big and scary. 37

"Only if you promise to hold my hand," said Oakey.

38

39

So Oakey's mom led him down the long lane.
Oakey wished he was back at home again!

"This looks like a great place to play.
Shall we take a look? What do you say?"
asked Oakey's mom.

"Only if you hold my hand," said Oakey.

42

And Oakey did it!

"Look at **me**! I can do it!" he cried.

"This slide looks like fun.
Would you like to try?"
asked Oakey's mom.

Oakey looked at the ladder. It **s t r e t c h e d**
44 right up to the sky.

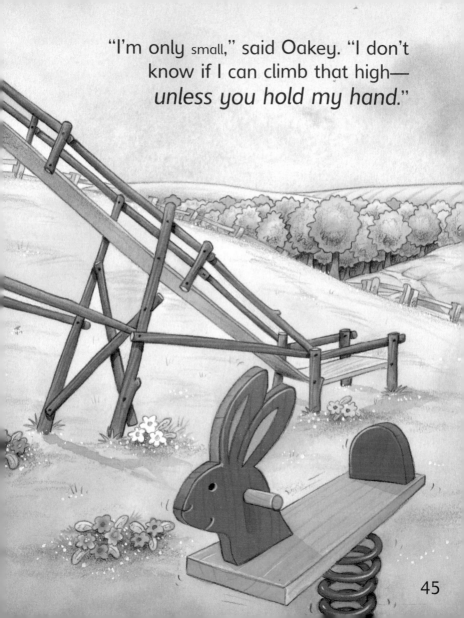

"I'm only small," said Oakey. "I don't know if I can climb that high— *unless you hold my hand.*"

And Oakey did it!

46

"Wheee! Did you see me?" he cried.

47

"We'll take a short cut through the wood," said Oakey's mom.

"I'm not sure if we should," said Oakey. "It looks dark in there. Well, I suppose we could—*will you hold my hand?*"

And Oakey did it!

"Boo! I scared you!" he cried.

Deep in the wood Oakey found a stream, shaded by beautiful tall trees.

52

"Stepping stones, look!"
said Oakey's mum.
"Do you think you could jump
across these?"

"Maybe," said
Oakey. "*I just need you
to hold my hand, please.*"

53

four...

three...

"Your turn now, Mom," cried Oakey,
holding out his hand.

Beyond the woods, Oakey and his mom
ran up the hill, and all the way
down to the ocean.

"Come on, Oakey," called his mom.

"Would you like to paddle in the sea with me?"

57

But the sea looked **big**, and he was only small.

Suddenly, Oakey knew that didn't matter at all. He turned to his mom and smiled...

59

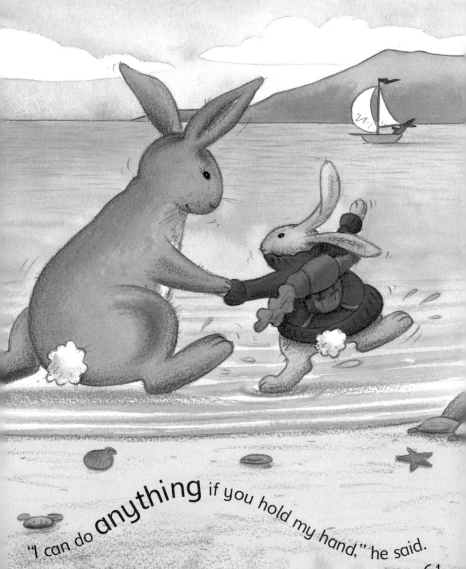

"I can do **anything** if you hold my hand," he said.

61

Just as Well, Really!

Rumpus liked water.

He liked the
drippiness and
droppiness,

the **splashiness**
and sloppiness
of it!

He liked it so much that, whenever there
was water around...

...Rumpus somehow always managed to—

66

But Mom loved Rumpus, so

...y time, she simply sighed—and she mopped up the mess.

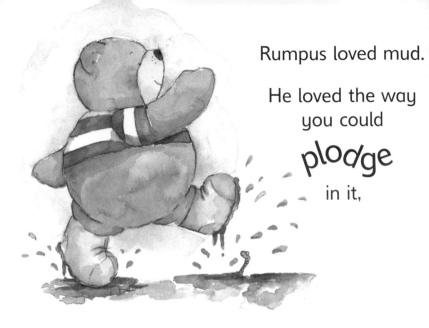

Rumpus loved mud.

He loved the way
you could

plodge

in it,

splodge
in it,
slide
in it and
glide
in it!

He loved it so much that, whenever there was mud around...

72

But Dad loved Rumpus, so

every time, he just sighed—and
he sponged off the splatters.

Rumpus enjoyed paint.

He liked to
splatter
and
dash it,

to spread
and
splash
it!

He enjoyed it so much that,
whenever there was paint around...

But Rumpus's brother loved him, so

every time, he just sighed—and he cleaned himself up.

Rumpus liked to find out how things worked.

He loved the prodding and probing,

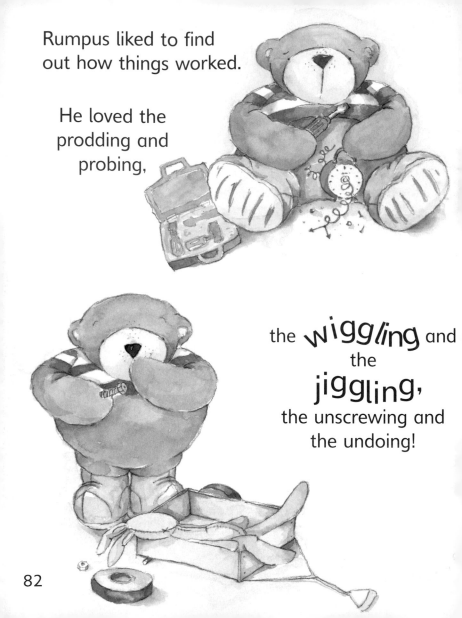

the **wiggling** and the **jiggling,** the unscrewing and the undoing!

...loved it so much that, whenever Rumpus was around...

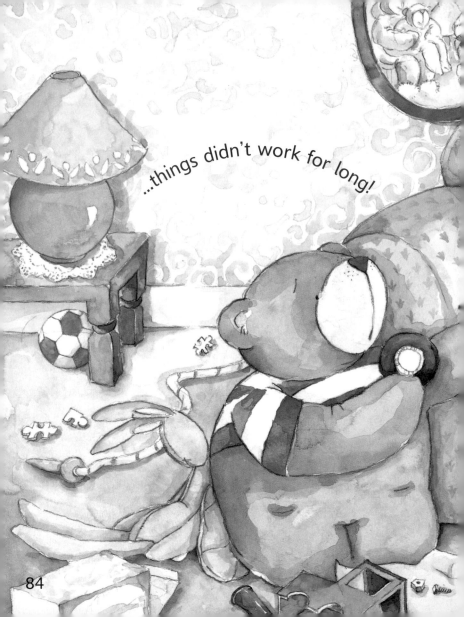

...things didn't work for long!

85

But Grandma loved Rumpus, so she just sighed—and she cleaned up the clutter.

Rumpus loved his
mom, dad...

brother, and grandma...

Rumpus's mom, dad, brother, and grandma loved Rumpus...

...just as well, really!

89

On my Own

Deep in the jungle, where only wild things go, Mungo's mom was teaching him what a young monkey needs to know. "Some things just aren't safe to try alone," she said.

"Why not?" said Mungo. "I'm big enough to do things—

on my own!"

93

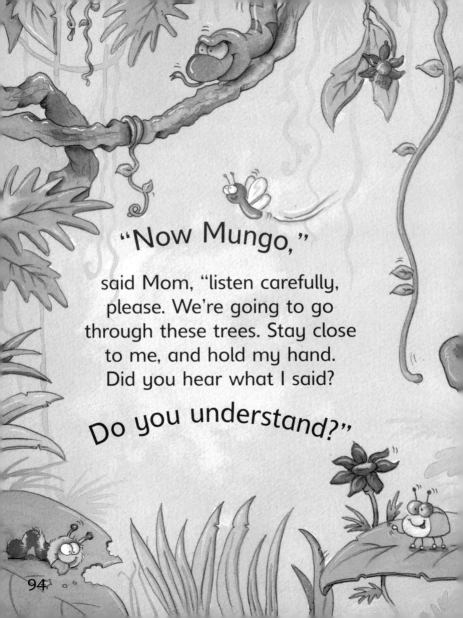

"Now Mungo,"

said Mom, "listen carefully, please. We're going to go through these trees. Stay close to me, and hold my hand. Did you hear what I said?

Do you understand?"

94

"It's okay, Mom. I won't slip or fall. I can swing across there with no trouble at all," said Mungo. "I'm big enough to do it— on my own!" And off he swung.

"Hissss,"
hissed Snake,
in a snake sort
of wail.

"That pesky Mungo
pulled my tail!"

98

And did Mungo hear poor old Snake groan?

No!
Mungo just laughed.
"I told you I could do it
on my own."

"Now, we're going to cross the river using these stones," said Mom. "But, Mungo, I'd rather you didn't do this alone."

100

"But Mom," said Mungo, and he ran on without stopping, "I'm really good at jumping and hopping. I'm big enough to do it—

on my own!"

102

And off he sprang!

103

"That Mungo trampled on my nose!" said Croc.

"Next time, I'll nibble off his toes!"
And did Mungo hear poor old Croc groan?
No! Mungo just smiled. "I told you I could do it
on my own."

105

"Mungo," said Mom, with a serious look on her face, "the jungle can be a dangerous place. There are all sorts of corners for creatures to hide, so, from now on, please stay by my side."

"Oh, Mom," said Mungo, "I don't need to wait for you. I can find my own way through. I'm big enough to do it— **on my own!**"

Lion rubbed the lump on his nose.

"Ouch!

That Mungo's so careless!" he said.
And did Mungo hear poor old Lion groan?
No! Mungo just grinned. "I told you I could do it
on my own."

"I think I've had enough for one day,"
Mom said. "So get going, little monkey!
Now it really is time for bed!"

It was Mungo's turn to let out a **gro**a**n**.
"I don't want to go to bed—
on my own!"
"Don't worry," said Mom. "Come on,
kiss me good night, and I promise I'll
hold you and cuddle you tight."

Lion roared, "Is that Mungo still awake?" "Yes!" snapped Crocodile.

116

"Lets help him go to sleep," hissed Snake.

And into the velvety, starry sky drifted
the sounds of a jungle lullaby.

117

Guess What I Want?

"Guess what I want?" said Ruff to Rufus.

"Something from me?" asked Rufus.

"Now, let me see—what could it be?"

"You've got to guess," said Ruff.

"You want me to tie a string to the moon, so you can pull it around like a giant balloon?" said Rufus.

123

"We could tie the moon
to the post of your bed,
to shine through the night
above your head."

124

"Would you really get me the moon?" asked Ruff.

"Well, it would be quite hard to climb up that high, but for you, of course, I'd give it a try," said Rufus.

"Guess again," laughed Ruff.

127

"You want me to catch you
a shining white star,
and capture its bright light
for you in a jar?"
said Rufus.

129

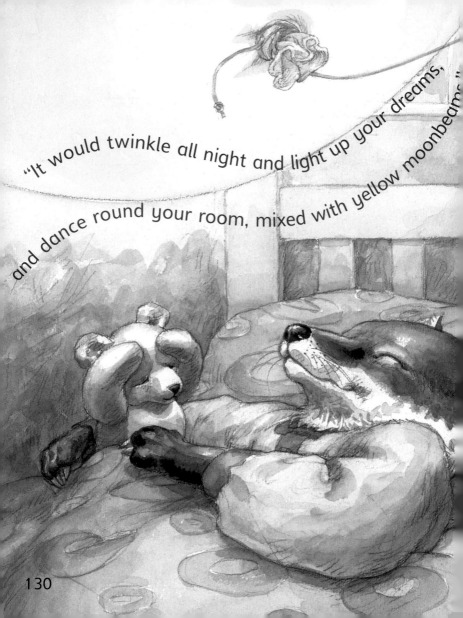

"It would twinkle all night and light up your dreams, and dance round your room, mixed with yellow moonbeams."

130

131

132

"Would you really fetch
me a star?" asked Ruff.

"Well, catching a star isn't easy to do,
but I'd give it a try,
because I love you," said Rufus.
"Guess again,"
laughed Ruff.

133

"You want me to capture the song of the breeze, as it lulls its way gently through leaves on the trees said Rufus.

134

"You'd be able to turn on the breeze's soft tune
for the starlight to dance along with the moon."

"Would you really bring me
the song of the breeze?" asked Ruff.

"Well, the breeze moves so fast, it isn't
easy to do, but I'd find a way to do it
for you," said Rufus.

140

Ruff thought hard.

"To tie down the moon, wouldn't be right. And the sky is the place to leave the starlight. It wouldn't be fair to stop the wind's song. Now, try one more guess—your first three were wrong!"

141

"I know. I was teasing
I think you want this.

142

143

...a huge great big cuddle, and a lovely big kiss!"

145

A Goodnight Kiss

"It's bedtime now, Oakey," said Mom.

148

Oakey curled up in the chair.
His ears began to droop and he muttered,
"Oh, that's not fair!"

"Have a drink first," smiled Mom, "then you must go."
"Five minutes more!" begged Oakey.
Mom answered, "No!"

100 recipes for CARROTS

150

Oakey's ears drooped and off he went.
But he was **back in a flash!**

"Where's your drink?" asked Mom.
"You haven't been very long.
You look scared, Oakey.
Is there something wrong?"

"There's a monster
in the kitchen,
with long, white shaggy hair,
lurking in the corner,
behind the rocking chair,"
said Oakey.

Mom laughed.
"Oh, Oakey, you've made a mistake.
That's no monster. It's a mop." And she gave the mo a shake.

154

Oakey's ears drooped
and off he went.
But he was
back in a flash!

"What's the matter?"
asked Mom.

"There's a ghost
in the hallway, hovering around.
Look, there it is floating
just above the ground,"
he wailed.

"Oh, Oakey, you've made a mistake.
That's no ghost.
It's just an old coat, hanging on
the hook.
Coats don't float!" laughed Mom.

158

Oakey's ears drooped and
off he went.
But he was
back in a flash!

"Why aren't you in bed, Oakey?"
asked Mom.

"There's a
great big lump
beneath the sheets.
It's waiting to get me.
I'm scared it's going to pounce.
Please come and see,"
sniffed Oakey.

160

"Oh, Oakey, you've made a mistake.
The only thing underneath the sheets,
is your old teddy bear," smiled Mom.

162

Oakey's ears drooped
and he got into bed.
But he didn't
close his eyes.

163

"Why aren't you asleep?"
asked Mom.

"There are
huge creepy crawlies
underneath my bed.
And I can't get the thought of them
out of my head,"
complained Oakey.

"They're just your slippers, Oakey, so there's no need to hide. They be won't creeping anywhere without your feet inside," grinned Mom.
"That's it now, Oakey. Time to say goodnight."

Mom turned and left the room, switching off the light.

And then Oakey saw it,
standing by the door.
The monster!

It moved across the floor and walked
straight towards him, with its arms
stretched out. Oakey's mouth opened,
but he found he couldn't shout.

The monster leaned over him and Oakey closed his eyes. What happened next gave Oakey an enormous surprise. The monster picked him up and cuddled him tight. Monsters just don't do that.

This couldn't be right!

Then Mom's voice whispered,
"Don't worry, it's just me.
When I said 'Goodnight' just now,
I forgot to give you this."

Then 'Monster Mom' gave Oakey
a goodnight kiss!

Kiss it Better

Rumpus was romping around the living room.
He cartwheeled across the carpet.

He turned a somersault on the sofa.

"Be careful!"
called Mom.

Too late! Rumpus slipped from the sofa, crumpled onto the carpet and banged his head on the floor.

178

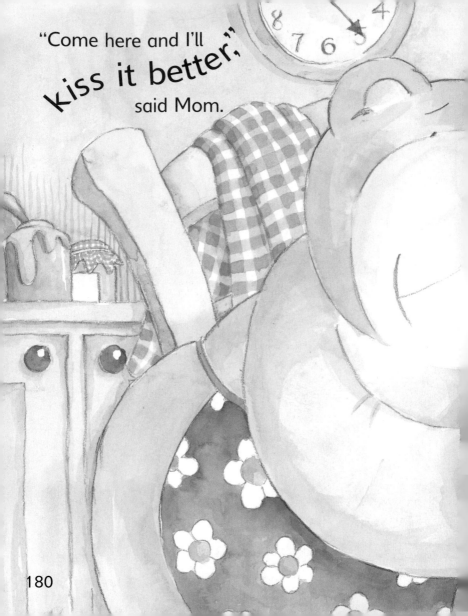

"Come here and I'll kiss it better," said Mom.

180

She hugged Rumpus and planted a kiss on his forehead.

"Now, go and find something less rowdy to do," she said.

Rumpus rushed out into the garden
and began to ride his bike.
Round and round he raced.

"Watch out!"
called Mom.

183

Too late!
Rumpus crashed into the corner of the wheelbarrow...

184

and tumbled to the
ground and grazed his knee.

"My leg hurts!"

he wailed. 185

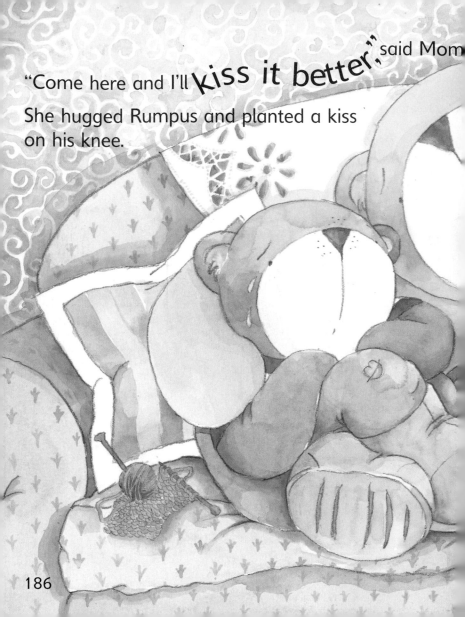

"Come here and I'll kiss it better," said Mom.

She hugged Rumpus and planted a kiss on his knee.

186

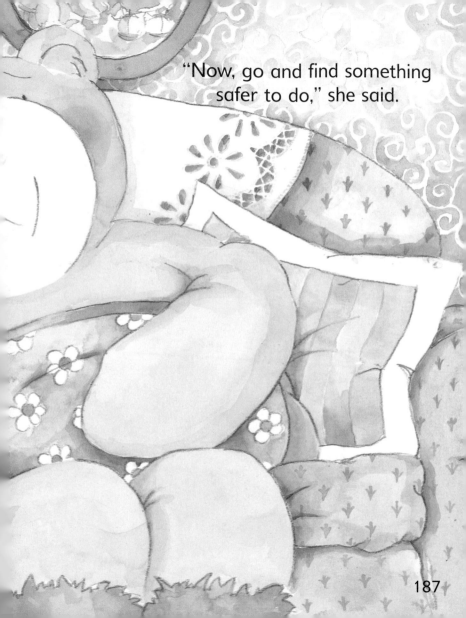

"Now, go and find something safer to do," she said.

Rumpus ran up the grassy slope.

Then he rolled down.

"Roly poly, down the hill," he sang.

"Look where you're going!"

called Mom.

Too late!

Rumpus rolled right into
the rose bush.
The thorns scratched him all
along his arm.

"My arm's sore!"
cried Rumpus.

"Come here and I'll **kiss *it better***", said Mom and she planted kisses all up his arm.

"Now, try and keep out of trouble," she said.

193

Mom went into the kitchen.
"I need a break,"
she thought.

194

She made a cup of tea.
She cut herself a slice of cake.
Then, she sat down for five minutes.

Just as she picked up her cup,
Rumpus zoomed into the kitchen...

on his **skateboard.**

"Rumpus!" said Mom.
"Can't you find something more sensible to do?"

197

Mom moved into the living room.
"I need a rest," she thought.
She sat down on the sofa and picked
up the paper.

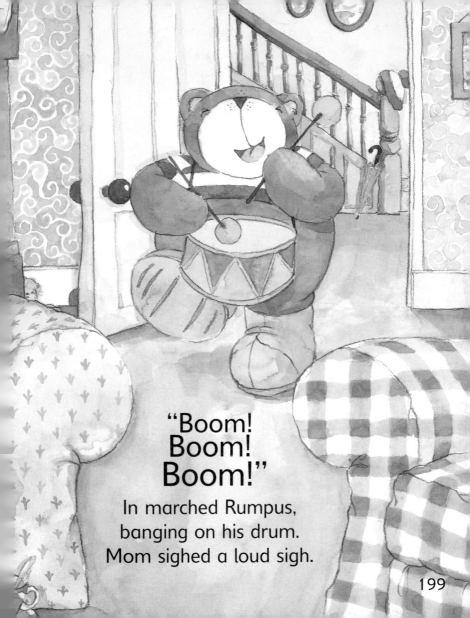

"Boom!
Boom!
Boom!"

In marched Rumpus,
banging on his drum.
Mom sighed a loud sigh.

199

"Is anything wrong?" asked Rumpus.
"I've got a headache!" said Mom.

"Never mind," smiled Rumpus, throwing his arms round her. "I'll soon kiss it better."

Lost and Alone

Deep in the jungle, Mungo was trying
to slip off through the trees.

"Mungo, tell me where you're going,
please," called Mom.

"What are you planning to do today?"

204

"I'm just going to play," smiled Mungo.
"Okay," said Mom.
"But no monkey business!"

205

"Easy" said Mungo. "All you have to do, is pull a funny face. Look, I'll show you."

And he took hold of Elephant's trunk.

Mungo wound Elephant's trunk round and round and slipped the end through.
He pulled it into a knot.

"Wow, Elephant!" he giggled.

"What a funny face you've got!"

"Hey!" gurgled Elephant. "How do I get out of this?"

But Mungo was gone!

Down by the river bank,
Crocodile was trying to nap,
when Mungo jumped out of the trees,
and gave his nose a tap.

"Want to play?" Mungo asked.

"I know a good game."

"Really?" said Crocodile,
suspiciously.
"What's its name?"

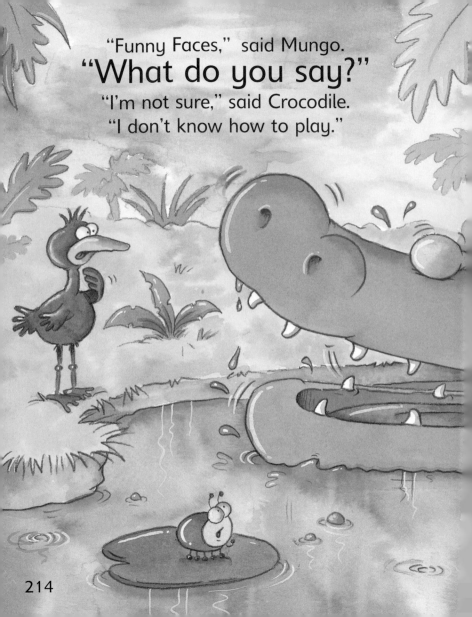

"Funny Faces," said Mungo.
"What do you say?"
"I'm not sure," said Crocodile.
"I don't know how to play."

"**Easy**," said Mungo. "All you have to do,
is pull a funny face. Look, I'll show you."
And he took hold of Crocodile's jaws.

215

Mungo pulled on one jaw, and pushed on the other.
Then he jammed them both together.

"Hey, Croc!" he giggled.
"That's a really funny face!"
"Help!" choked Crocodile. "How do I get
out of this?"
But Mungo was gone!

Lion was trying to have a laze in the sun, when Mungo swung down and asked, **"Want some fun?"** Then he added, "Come on. I know a good game."

"Yeah?" said Lion, suspiciously. "What's its name?"

"Funny Faces,"
said Mungo.
**"What do
you say?"**
"I'm not sure," said Lion.
"I don't know how to play."

"Easy," said Mungo.
"All you have to do, is pull a
funny face. Look, I'll show you."

And he took hold of
Lion's bottom lip.

Mungo pulled the lip up over Lion's nose.
"You see," he said, "that's the way it goes."

Then he ran off, smiling, through the trees.
"Forget what Mom said," thought Mungo.
"I'll do as I please."
He swung through the branches, but, after a while,
Mungo's face lost its smile.

"I don't know where I am!" he wailed.

"That's a funny face," said Elephant.
"He wins the game for sure."
"You're right," laughed Lion.
"Come on, Mungo, give us more."

224

"Well, shall we help him?" Lion roared.
"What do you think?"

"I'm not sure," said Elephant.
"He did disturb my drink."

"And he woke me up," Crocodile complained,
"which really wasn't fun."

"He wrecked my rest, too," Lion said.
"You're not the only one."

227

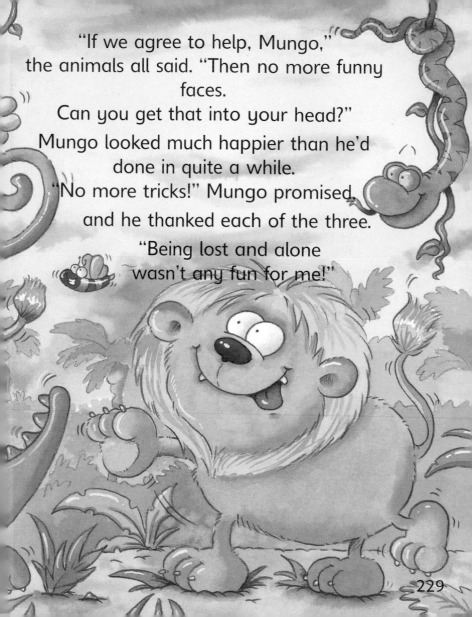

"If we agree to help, Mungo,"
the animals all said. "Then no more funny
faces.
Can you get that into your head?"

Mungo looked much happier than he'd
done in quite a while.
"No more tricks!" Mungo promised,
and he thanked each of the three.

"Being lost and alone
wasn't any fun for me!"

This is a Parragon Publishing Book
This edition published in 2003

Parragon Publishing
Queen Street House,
4 Queen Street,
Bath BA1 1HE, UK.

Created by The Complete Works
Written by Jillian Harker
Illustrated by Andy Everitt-Stewart,
Louise Gardner, Julie Nicholson and Pamela Venus

ISBN 0-75258-911-3
Printed in China